JN013358

前田万葉句集

かまくら春秋社

Haiku of Manyo Maeda

Kamakura Shunju-sha Co., Ltd

前田万葉句集

Haiku of Manyo Maeda

前田神父様の句は
伝達と表現と信仰が融合して心に届きます。

夏井いつき

Cardinal Maeda's haiku touch the heart
with their fusion of communication, expression, and faith.

Itsuki Natsui

カバー画　北見隆
装丁　中村聡

Cover Illustration by Takashi Kitami
Book Design by Satoshi Nakamura

目次

Contents

まえがき

前田万葉

私の万葉（まんよう）という名前が普通ではないので子どもの頃、友達からよくからかわれました。そのことは先に出版した自著の中でも書きました。でもその名前がこの度の句集の誕生の幸運をもたらしたのです。

長崎県佐世保市のカトリック俵町教会に赴任した時に、当時の小教区評議会の議長であった嶋田政美様（俳号＝乱雪）から、「万葉という名前はそのまま俳号になりますから一緒に俳句を作りましょう」と誘われ俳句を作りはじめました。

その中の一句「烏賊墨の一筋垂れて冬の弥撒」が編集者・伊藤玄二郎様の目に留まり、一冊の本が世に出ました。とても嬉しいことでした。このことが縁となり今回の初の句集を編むことになりました。畏敬する黒田杏子さんが心のこもった解説を書いてくださり感謝でいっぱいです。これもひとえに、伊藤様のお誘いで、月刊「かまくら春秋」の「俳句を語る」座談会でご一緒させていただいた賜物です。おまけに、私の句を二句も添削していただくという、貴重な体験もできました。

さらに帯は今や国民的人気を誇る夏井いつきさんからいただきました。夏井さんとは、同じ座談会の中で、子どもの頃の海の体験が意気投合し、ますます俳句に熱が入ります。こんな幸せは人生の中でそうあるものではありません。私には分不相応なことに思われますが、これも神様のお導きとありがたく受け止めております。

前作に続き、カバー画を描いてくださった北見隆様にも感謝申し上げます。私の生い立ちや生活そのものを表現してくださっているようで、心和みます。あわせて、拙句を英訳いただいたジェームス・ケティング様にも感謝申し上げます。

二〇二〇年六月

This, too, would not have occurred had it not been for Mr. Ito, who invited us to come together and discuss haiku. In addition, I had the precious experience of watching Ms. Kuroda examine, and suggest corrections to, two of my haiku while there.

The haiku poet Itsuki Natsui, who now commands a nationwide popularity, graciously agreed to write text for the obi band for this book. At the same gathering, she and I hit it off quite well because of our shared childhood experiences by the sea. Meeting her has made me even more enthusiastic about haiku composition. Such a happy chain of events is not very common in this life. I feel that it is more than I deserve, but am taking it as another instance of divine guidance and gladly accepting it.

I must also express my thanks to Takashi Kitami, who produced the illustration on the front cover, as he did for my previous book. His illustration gives me a warm feeling; it looks like a depiction of my childhood and very life itself. Thanks are likewise due to James Koetting for the English translation of this book.

June 2020

Foreword

When I was a child, I was often teased by my friends because "Manyo," my given name, was out of the ordinary. I also mentioned this in my previous book. This name, however, brought me good luck, for it eventually resulted in the birth of this haiku collection.

When I was sent to Tawaramachi Church in the city of Sasebo, Nagasaki Prefecture, Masami Shimada (whose pen name is "Ransetsu"), who was then chairman of the parish council, asked me to compose haiku with him, adding, "the name 'Manyo' makes a nice pen name as is." And that is when I started to make haiku.

One of my haiku went: I rush back to port / Wearing a streak of squid ink / Winter morning mass. This caught the eye of Genjiro Ito, the editor of "Kamakura Shunju," and a book I authored was published as a result. I was really gladdened by the publication, and my acquaintance with Mr. Ito subsequently led to the preparation of this first collection of my haiku. The haiku poet Momoko Kuroda, whom I positively revere, wrote a lovely commentary on the collection, and I am filled with gratitude to her for it.

前田万葉句集

俳句

Haiku of Manyo Maeda

Haiku

秋の灯やミサからミサへ親も子も

ミサに参加する親子の姿があります。カトリック信者にとって、生活、活動の頂点はミサなのです。神と隣人に対してお互いゆるしをこい、御言葉に励まされ御聖体に強められて、また一日の生活に活動に宣教にと、つかわされる恵みの泉なのです。

Aki no hi ya
misa kara misa e
oya mo ko mo

In autumn candle light
Living life from mass to mass
Both parent and child

Parents and their children attend mass. For each of us Catholics, the mass is at the summit of our lives and activities. Through it, we ask God and our neighbor for forgiveness, are heartened by the words of the Lord, and strengthened by the Eucharist. It is the font of the grace we need for our daily life, activities, and mission.

ありがたく命生きよとクリスマス

神様からいただいた命です。クリスマスの日、改めて命の尊さを考えてみましょう。神の子キリストが、人間とまで生(な)ってくださり、共に寄り添ってくださるのです。

Arigataku
inochi ikiyo to
kurisumasu

Oh so gratefully To be lived, this gift of life Thoughts on Christmas day

Our God-given life. Christmas is a fitting time to once again recall its preciousness. Christ, the Son of God, even became a human being and will stay close to us.

回心と恵みの時や四旬節

四旬節は罪を悔い、償うために回心し、さまざまな社会的問題についても改める恵のときです。共に痛みを分かち合い、神に心を向け直して生活も改めましょう。

Kaishin to
megumi no toki ya
shijunsetsu

A soul-searching time
Repentance and charity
The Lenten season

Lent is a period of contrition for our sins and a change of heart for atonement. It is also a time for acts of benevolence to help resolve various social issues. I ask the faithful to use it to share pain, turn our hearts to God, and better our lives.

難民の如し鴉樹に群るる

教会の集まりに車を走らせていた時のことです。街路樹に群れる鴉が、私にはあのボート難民の姿と重なりました。鴉の群れが哀れに思われてなりませんでした。

Nanmin no

gotoshi hiyodori

ki ni mururu

Like war's refugees
Flocks of brown-eared
bulbul birds
Roosting in the trees

It was when I was driving to a gathering at the church. The many bulbuls that were perched in the roadside trees caught my eye and reminded me of refugees trying to flee war in boats. I couldn't help feeling sorry for the flocks of birds.

Note: The "hiyodori," or brown-eared bulbul, is a migratory songbird found in rural and urban areas throughout Japan.

母の日や母から母へまた母へ

母の日は母に感謝する日です。本当はこちらからご馳走してあげなくてはいけないのです。私の母は「レストランなんか行かなくてもいい」と、その日も台所に立ってくれ、私は母の手料理を楽しんだものです。そのように、「おふくろの味」は伝わっていくのでしょう。

Haha no hi ya
haha kara haha e
mata haha e

Mother's Day arrives
Mother succeeding mother
Then comes another

Mother's Day is a day for thanking your mother. Actually, we should be treating our mothers to dinner. My mother would say there was no need to go to a restaurant, and make dinner herself, so I enjoyed her homemade dishes on that day as well. That's how a mother's cooking is passed on.

父の日や親子三代晩酌す

一九八〇年代、平戸市では養豚が盛んでした。この句の人は、豚を市場に運ぶ仕事をしています。一家は祖父母・両親・子どもの三代が同居しています。たまの休みになると家族で魚釣りを楽しみます。私はその人の家で釣った魚を、一四人の大家族と一緒に食べお酒を飲むのが楽しみでした。

Chichi no hi ya
oyako sandai
banshaku su

The Father's Day fete
Three generations gather
Sipping drinks at eve

In the 1980s, pig-farming was prevalent in Hirado. The man who inspired this haiku does the work of hauling pigs to the market. When he gets some time off, he likes to go fishing. I enjoyed drinking with at his place while dining on fish he caught at feasts with all 14 members of his family.

Note: Historic Hirado City is located on Hirado Island, the 4th largest of the islands off the coast of Nagasaki. Because of changes to the city's boundaries, Hirado City now includes parts of the main island of Kyushu.

子どもたち来たれうれしや夏休み

子どもたちが待ち焦がれた夏休みです。教会は、早朝ミサなどに子どもたちが集まり、にぎやかになります。これを私も待ちわびていたのです。

Kodomo tachi
ki tare ureshi ya
natsuyasumi

Gratifying days
Many children come to mass
Summer vacation

The summer vacation which the children have been anxiously waiting for. The church is filled with the voices of those who have come there for masses, starting with the early morning one. This is something I have been anxiously waiting for.

空の鳥野の花見よと春が来る

空を飛ぶ鳥が春の訪れを教えてくれます。なんと花に飾られた春の野は美しいのでしょう。聖書の一節が、聞こえてきます。「思い悩むな。空の鳥を見よ。野の花を見よ。明日のことは明日自らが思い悩む」と。

Sora no tori
no no hana miyo to
haru ga kuru

See the birds above
And the flowers in the field
Springtime's arrival

Birds flying across the sky tell us of spring's arrival. How beautiful the fields look adorned with flowers! I recall some words from the Bible: "Don't worry. Look at the birds in the sky. Look at the flowers in the field. Tomorrow will take care of itself."

十字切る人の末期に時雨けり

臨終に際して、薄れいく意識の中で十字架を切れる人は何と幸いな人でしょう。その枕辺に静かに時雨の音が届きます。

Jūji kiru
hito no matsugo ni
shigure keri

The sign of the cross
As he lay on his deathbed
A late autumn rain

How blessed are those who can make the sign of the cross as their consciousness fades in their final hours! At bedside, I could hear the sound of a late autumn rain softly falling.

笹鳴くや目覚めうらはら朝の雨

心地よい目覚めが、笹鳴きと共に訪れました。なのに表は雨です。講演会場に来場を予定されている多くの信者さんが足を運んでくれるか心配です。（でも会場は多くの信者さんで大混雑。嬉しい悲鳴でした。）

Sasa naku ya
mezame urahara
asa no ame

A bush warbler's song
But waking I discover
A morning shower

A pleasant waking came with the twittering of a bush warbler. But outside, it was raining. I was worried about whether the many faithful who were supposed to come to my lecture would actually make the journey to the venue. (But as things turned out, the venue was packed. I was happy in spite of the extra work this meant.)

ひさかたの雪の清さよ平戸島

久し振りに平戸に泊まりました。夜、先輩の神父さんと夜を徹して酌み交わしました。話題は平戸の激しい選挙戦や湾岸戦争。暗いものでした。でも朝、目を覚ますと窓の外は銀世界。心が清められた気持ちになりました。

Hisakata no
yuki no kiyosa yo
hiradojima

After a long spell
The purity of snowfall
Hirado island

I was staying in Hirado after a long interval. That night, I drank until late with an older priest. We talked about the fiercely fought election in Hirado and the Gulf War. Some depressing subjects. But when I opened my eyes in the morning, the world outside the window was cloaked in white. I felt as if my heart and mind had been cleansed.

法王衣の清さよ雪に染りけり

平戸の久し振りの雪に一〇年前の教皇ヨハネ・パウロ二世が長崎を訪れた日のことを思い出していました。長崎は雪でした。法王の白い法衣は雪の輝きで、さらに白く清らかに映じていました。

Hōōi no
kiyosa yo yuki ni
somari keri

The papal vestment
Immaculateness sparkling
Melting specks of snow

As the first snow in a long time fell in Hirado, I recalled the day when Pope John Paul II visited Nagasaki 10 years earlier. It snowed in Nagasaki on that day. The Pope's white robe looked even whiter and purer with the sparkle of the snowflakes.

戦争は死ですと聞こゆ吹雪かな

戦争は人間の仕業です。戦争は人間の生命の破壊です。戦争は死です。吹きすさぶ雪の中からあのヨハネ・パウロ二世の声が聞こえてきます。

Sensō wa
shi desu to kiko yu
fubuki kana

War only brings death
I could hear the pontiff say
Despite the blizzard

Wars are made by human beings. Wars are the destruction of people's lives. Wars are death. I could hear the voice of Pope John Paul II, even through the blowing, swirling snow.

平和をと切磋琢磨や時鳥

元外務大臣安倍晋太郎氏が亡くなりました。五、六年前、私は佐世保市で安倍外相の講演会に参加し、その内政・外交姿勢や人柄に感動したものです。特にアフリカ飢餓救済を訴え、国民にその輪を広げたのは素晴らしいものでした。それはライバルであった竹下登氏との互いに引き上げ合って競い合う中で生まれたと聞いています。

Hēwa o to
sessatakuma ya
hototogisu

For peace in the world
All working hard together
Cuckoo's summer cry

Former Minister of Foreign Affairs Shintaro Abe passed away. Five or six years before his death, I heard him speak in the city of Sasebo, and was deeply moved by his stance on domestic and foreign affairs, and by his character. His call for the provision of relief for hunger in Africa and widening of this circle of concern to involve the people of Japan were particularly wonderful. I understand that this came about in the context of the friendly competition with Noboru Takeshita, his rival.

九条は十字架という終戦日

日本国民が立憲の精神、初心を忘れ、経済繁栄に溺れて、目先の物的豊かさや国際世論にだけ気をとられていると、肝心の一番大切な平和を忘れてしまう恐れがあります。九条はまさに十字架です。これによって平和は保たれているのです。

Kyūjō wa

jūjika to iu

shūsembi

The ninth article Like a promise on the cross End of the War Day

If the people of Japan forget the spirit and intent behind the constitution, drown in economic prosperity, and concern themselves solely with material affluence and international opinion, they are liable to lose sight of the most important, vital thing they have - peace. Article 9 of the constitution is exactly like a cross safeguarding peace.

六坪牢いまも窄には汗の列

明治政府のキリシタン弾圧に久賀島の信徒らが捕えられ、わずか六坪の牢屋に老若男女二〇〇余人が監禁され四二人が殉教しました。今でも牢屋の窄には猛暑の中でも流れ落ちる汗もいとわず、清掃やミサが続けられています。

Rokutsuborō

ima mo sako ni wa

ase no retsu

Only six tsubo
The prison still cramped today
Perspiring faithful

In the wave of oppression of Christians by the Meiji government, believers on Hisakajima Island were arrested and imprisoned. More than 200 people, both men and women, and young and old, were held in a jail measuring only about six "tsubo" (roughly 20 square meters), and 42 of them died for their faith. Today as well, people come to the jail for cleaning and masses even in sweltering heat, cramped, sweaty space.

Note: Hisakajima Island is one of the islands in the Goto archipelago, Nagasaki Prefecture. The Goto Islands sheltered many "hidden" Christians.

蟬時雨止みて園児の声となり

毎日、蟬時雨で始まっていた朝が、突然、園児の元気な声がこだまします。「おはよう」「おはよう」。夏休みが終わり二学期が始まったのです。

Semishigure
yami te enji no
koe to nari

Kindergarten yard
When cicada droning stops
Children's voices heard

The mornings were always filled with the drone of cicadas, but all of a sudden, the air now resounds with the spirited cries of children. "Good morning!" "Yeah, good morning!" It is the end of summer vacation and the start of the second term.

泣き笑ふ童のほっぺ花の舞

サン・テグジュペリは「かつて子どもだったことを忘れずにいる人はいくらもいない」と嘆いています。いつまでも子ども心を忘れて欲しくないものです。イエス曰く、「子どものようにならなければ天の国に入ることはできない」と。

Nakiwarau

warabe no hoppe

hana no mai

On cheeks of children
Both laughing and shedding tears
Fallen petals stuck

Saint-Exupéry lamented, "All grown-ups were once children... but only few of them remember it." I never want to forget my childhood heart. Jesus said: "Unless you turn and become like children, you will not enter the kingdom of heaven."

ままごとに神の声して秋うらら

ままごとをしている子どもたちの声が聞こえます。「食事は家族みんなでしましょうね」「お母さんは子どもが帰る時はお家でお迎えしてね」そんな神様の声も聞こえます。

Mamagoto ni
kami no koe shite
aki urara

**Children's mimicry
Is joined by a voice divine
Glorious autumn**

I can hear the children playing house. I also seem to hear a divine voice saying things such as, "It's good for the whole family to eat meals together" and "Mothers should be at home to greet children when they come back from school."

村中が段々畑麦を蒔く

私が子どもの頃、村人（長崎県新上五島町仲知）の主食は麦でした。狭い段々畑で麦蒔きや麦踏みを手伝ったものです。

Murajū ga
dandambatake
mugi o maku

Every villager
At work in the terraced fields
Sowing seeds of wheat

When I was a child, wheat was a staple food of the people in our community (in the district of Chuchi, Shin-Kami-Goto-cho, Nagasaki Prefecture). I helped with the work of sowing wheat seeds on the narrow terraced fields and treading the plants.

Note: Treading seedlings, known as "mugifumi," was long practiced in Japan. Stressing seedlings strengthens the roots and increases yields. Shin-Kami-Goto town forms the north part of the Goto Archipelago.

うしろ手に母のまねして麦を踏む

麦踏みにはコツがあります。丁寧に愛情を込めて踏まねばなりません。母は子どもを背負っているように腰の後ろに手を組んで丁寧に麦踏みをしていました。その格好が愛情そのもののように見えました。

Ushirode ni
haha no mane shite
mugi o fumu

Hands behind my back
Imitating my mother
Treading plants of wheat

There is a certain trick to treading wheat. You must stamp on the plants with care and love. My mother carefully treaded them while clasping her hands behind her, as if carrying a baby on her back. The figure she cut when treading wheat looked like love itself to me.

一粒の踏まれし麦やキリスト忌

イエスはご自分の受難と死、そして栄光を（一粒の麦に）たとえて語りました。「一粒の麦は、地に落ちて死ななければ、一粒のままである。だが、死ねば、多くの実を結ぶ」。

Hitotsubu no
fumareshi mugi ya
kirisutoki

Seedling wheat stamped down
A single grain drops to earth
Memento Christi

Jesus likened his own suffering, death, and glory to a single grain of wheat. He said: "Unless a grain of wheat falls to the ground and dies, it remains just a grain of wheat; but if it dies, it produces much fruit."

「えらい」とは「きつい」ことかよ朝の汗

キリストは「あなたがたの中でえらくなりたい者は皆に仕える者になりなさい」と言っています。仕えるとはきつい、今で言う３Ｋを伴います。キリストの生涯も３Ｋであり、それは十字架の道でした。実際に、「きつい」時に、「えらい」と言われたことがありました。

Erai to wa
kitsui koto ka yo
asa no ase

Ah, by "outstanding" He meant "tough" work in the barn! Sweat in morning

Christ said, "Whoever wishes to be great among you shall become your servant." To serve can be tough. It is accompanied by what is called "3K" work (in English, it would be "3D," standing for dirty, dangerous, and/or demanding). Christ's life was 3K; it was the way of the cross. In fact, I was once called "outstanding" at a "tough" time.

マリア笑む銀杏黄葉の天主堂

この銀杏の木は「落葉がひどく掃除に面倒。教会が見えにくい」。こんな理由で切り倒されようとしていました。しかし、教会外の予期せぬ人から良さを指摘され、俵町教会のシンボルとして頑張っています。人は一つだけの物の見方で価値を決めてはならないのです。また、木にも魂があるのです。

Maria emu
ichō momiji no
tenshudō

Virgin Mary smiles
A ginkgo tree's golden leaves
Fallen on church grounds

Some people wanted to cut down this tree, complaining that its fallen leaves were hard to rake up and it partially hid the church. This was prevented, however, when people outside the church unexpectedly pointed out its good features. The tree continues to stand as the symbol of Tawaramachi Church. We must not decide the value of something from just one perspective. And trees, too, have a soul.

Note: Catholic Tawaramachi Church is in the Sasebo area of Nagasaki Prefecture.

バラ挿して父親たちはミサの中

「なぜ父の日にバラか」とミサの中で説教をしました。「バラにはトゲがあるように、父親の愛には厳しさがなければならない」ということを言いたかったのです。

出版のご案内

株式会社かまくら春秋社

写真文化首都「写真の町」
東川町・発行　●各1800円＋税

セイ、町の魅力など。

富山市・発行　●2500円＋税

売薬、用具や人々などを紹介。

子どもに贈りたい絵本&かるた

こうちゃんの氷川丸

文／田村朗　絵／吉野晃希男　●1400円＋税

横浜のシンボル氷川丸を訪れたこうちゃんが出会ったのは――。

ベイリーとさっちゃん

文／田村朗　絵／粟冠ミカ　●1600円＋税

絵本「ベイリー物語」刊行実行委員会・発行

病院に常勤して病気の子どもをささえる医療スタッフ犬「ベイリー」。ファシリティドッグの存在をもっと知ってほしい、そんな願いで絵本になりました。

りんご

●1400円＋税

日英対訳

文／三木卓　絵と翻訳／スーザン・バーレイ

三木卓と、『わすれられないおくりもの』のスーザン・バーレイによる日英合作絵本。

オーロラのもえた夜

日・フィンランド・英語対訳　●1400円＋税

文／三木卓　原作・絵／キルシー・クラウディア・カンガス

ラップランド地方の伝承をもとにした、オーロラの物語。

3人はなかよしだった

文／三木卓　●1400円＋税

原作・絵／ケルットゥ・ヴオラッブ　英訳／ケイト・エルウッド　日英対訳

北極圏の先住民・サーミ人の文化を紹介する絵本。

フィンランドの森から

ヘイッキはおとこの子　日英対訳　●1400円＋税

文／三木卓　絵／ヴィーヴィ・ケンパイネン　英訳／飯田深雪

フィンランドの森を舞台にしたおとこの子の成長物語。

小さいうさぎと大都会

文／小池昌代　●1800円＋税

原作・絵／ディアーナ・カイヤカ　日英対訳

バルト海に面する国ラトビアから届いた心あたたまる物語。

鎌倉かるた

●1429円＋税

鎌倉ペンクラブ編

遊びながら鎌倉の歴史や文化が学べる、子どもから大人まで楽しめるかるた。絵札は、鎌倉在住の画家、作家らが手掛ける。

●価格表示は本体価格＋税（消費税）です

やなせたかしの本

歯科詩集
やなせたかし ●1200円+税
監修・日本歯科医師会会長 大久保満男

親子で楽しめるユニークな「歯」の詩だけの詩画集。日本歯科医師会会長監修で、歯の知識が身につくQ&A付き。

あなたも詩人 だれでも詩人になれる本
やなせたかし ●1200円+税

「へたも詩のうち。心にひびけばいい」。「手のひらを太陽に」の作詞者、やなせたかしが詩の読み方と、書き方を指南。

たそがれ詩集
やなせたかし ●1500円+税

九十歳で、「詩とファンタジー」に連載した詩を中心にまとめた大活字詩画集。じんわりとこころに沁みる作品集。

アホラ詩集
やなせたかし ●1500円+税

九十四歳で没する直前にまとめられた大活字詩画集第二弾。アンパンマンの作者が残した心に響く詩篇たち。

文化・外交関連書籍

ミネルヴァのふくろうと明日の日本
近藤誠一 ●1800円+税

3・11からの真の復興には文化・芸術の力こそ必要とする著者の考えに共鳴する画家たちが挿絵を添えた画文集。

外交官のア・ラ・カルト ―文化と食を巡る外交エッセイ―
近藤誠一 ●1800円+税

前文化庁長官の著者が、外交官時代に出合った数々の食文化。「食」を手がかりに外交の真髄に迫る一冊。

Bara sashite
chichioya tachi wa
misa no naka

A rose in a vase
For fathers on Father's Day
A thorny sermon

"Why roses on Father's Day?" I spoke on this question in my sermon during mass. I wanted to tell the fathers present that, just as roses have thorns, a father's love must contain sternness.

晩鐘のごとしモロコシ刈る農夫

私が田平教会を最初に訪れた時、突然、目の前に現れたのは、まさにあのミレーの名画「晩鐘」の舞台であるかのような錯覚を受けるほど、のどかな田園風景の中のレンガ造りの教会でした。そして実にアンゼラスの鐘が似合うような教会でした。

Banshō no

gotoshi morokoshi

karu nōfu

Like an angelus
Harvesting a sorghum crop
Tabira farmers

When I made my first visit to Tabira Church, what suddenly appeared before my eyes was an idyllic landscape right out of "The Angelus," the famous painting by Millet. The church was made of brick and sat in the middle of this scene. It really did make a fitting church for the angelus.

山歩く鹿と聖堂の見ゆるまで

前になったり、後ろになったり、鹿と歩いている内に、先祖らが造った野崎聖堂が目の前に現れました。人はいなく、さらに多くの鹿たちが歓迎してくれました。

Yama aruku
shika to midō no
miyuru made

**Hiking through the hills
With deer accompanying
Look! Ahead, the church!**

The deer appeared in the woods, sometimes to the front, sometimes to the rear. While proceeding along the path with them, there came into view Nozaki Seido, the church built by our ancestors. There was no one around, and even more deer were nearby to greet us.

ご無礼の申し訳なく年賀かな

皆様には、日ごろから物心両面でお世話になりながら、お礼の言葉、感謝の気持ちも表わさず、失礼いたしていますことをおゆるし下さい。年賀のご挨拶をかねて心からお詫び申し上げげます。

Goburei no
mōsiwakenaku
nenga kana

For being thoughtless
Offering apologies
My New Year's greeting

I would like to ask all to please forgive me for thoughtlessly neglecting to express my feelings of thanks in words, in spite of being so indebted to you for your material and moral support. My heartfelt apologies, along with greetings for the New Year!

ザビエルのお礼一筆夜長かな

一九九九年はザビエル日本渡来四五〇年。私たちの平戸地区を中心に記念行事が行われました。たくさんの人たちのご協力を頂きました。秋の夜長にお礼の手紙を書きましたが、行き届かずお詫びを申し上げる次第です。

Zabieru no
orei ippitsu
yonaga kana

Writing notes of thanks
Xavier celebration
Long the autumn nights

The year 1999 marked the 450th anniversary of Xavier's arrival in Japan. Events to celebrate this occasion were held mainly in our Hirado district, and garnered the cooperation of many people. I wrote letters of thanks on the long autumn nights, but also want to apologize for any shortcomings.

飼い葉桶餌と成しか神の御子

馬小屋が出来上がると空っぽの飼い葉桶が幼子の降誕を待ちます。いや、私たち一人一人を待っているのかもしれません。イエスと共に小さい者、そして人々の食べ物になるようにと。

Kaibaoke
esa to nari shi ka
kami no miko

The crib in the stable
Perhaps food for all of us
The infant Jesus

Once the stable is finished, the empty manger awaits the Nativity. Or perhaps it is waiting for each of us - to become like the infant Jesus and provide little ones and others with sustenance.

わら小屋と折り鶴ツリーや年迎ふ

旧年はキリスト生誕二〇〇〇年の聖年でした。田平教会では馬小屋をわらぶき小屋にして、巡礼者に折り鶴を捧げていただき、クリスマスツリーとして飾りました。新しい年を愛と祈りの年にしたいものです。

Waragoya to
orizuru tsurī ya
toshi mukau

With straw-thatched stable
Paper cranes for
Christmas trees
We greet the new year

The last year was a holy one marking the 2,000th anniversary of the birth of Christ. At Tabira Church, we built a stable with a straw-thatched roof, and had visiting pilgrims fold paper cranes that we displayed like Christmas trees. I hope to make the new year one of love and prayer.

千年と百年またぐ去年今年

今年から来年は二つの千年紀と百年紀を跨ぎます。この記念すべき旧・新紀に生きている恵みを感謝して、新しい二十一世紀が平和でありますように、と祈ります。

Sen nen to
hyaku nen matagu
kozo kotoshi

A millennium
And century we straddle
From last year to this one

As we go from this year into next year, we are entering both a new millennium and a new century. I am grateful for the blessing of living to see this momentous change of old and new ages, and pray that the new 21st century will bring peace.

ごきげんよう夫婦燕の宙返り

田平教会司祭館南門に巣作りをしていた夫婦燕は、私を平戸教会まで見送って来て一晩、聖堂の中に泊まりました。翌日の平戸教会での初ミサの最中に聖堂内を宙返り。チュチュチュと共に賛美の祈りを捧げて帰って行きました。無事に田平に戻って子育てをしているでしょうか。

Gokigenyō
meoto tsubame no
chūgaeri

I bid a farewell
The swallow pair, taking wing
Somersault in air

A pair of swallows built a nest on the south gate of the parsonage at Tabira Church. They used to see me off on my way to the church. One evening, they stayed inside the church. On the next morning, in the middle of the first mass, they suddenly took wing. Making a somersault, they flew away while tweeting what seemed like a hymn of praise. I wondered if they safely returned and are raising offspring in Tabira.

風鈴や寺院と教会鐘が鳴る

平戸の寺院と教会の見える風景の中にいると、方々からの鐘が音色を奏でる風鈴のように、心地よいものです。

Fūrin ya
jiin to kyōkai
kane ga naru

Like a wind chime's tune
Bells of temples and churches
Ringing together

Various temples and churches can be seen in the Hirado landscape. The rings of their different bells seem like a wind chime making a lovely melody. It gives you a pleasant feeling.

ガンバレとマリアの里の桜かな

四月三日、潮見教会の境内に入りました。突然強い風が吹き、桜の花が一輪、私の頬を打ちました。東京勤務最初の日、北原怜子マリア様の「ガンバレ」の励ましでしょうか。

注　エリザベト・マリア・北原怜子（一九二九―一九五八）は、「蟻の町のマリア」と呼ばれた人物。二〇一五年に遺徳がローマ教皇フランシスコにより認められた。

Gambare to
maria no sato no
sakura kana

Don't give up, she says
Where Maria helped the poor
Cherry trees in bloom

On April 3, I entered the grounds of Shiomi Church. All at once, there was a strong gust of wind, and a cherry blossom hit me on the cheek. It was my first day of service in Tokyo, and I felt the blossom was Maria Satoko Kitahara's way of urging me on.

Note: Elisabeth Maria Satoko Kitahara (1929-1958) was known as the "Mary of Ari-no-Machi". Ari-no-Machi (Ant Town) was a slum in what is now Sumida Ward, Tokyo. She was venerated in 2015 by Pope Francis.

調和する自然は神や野分波

まだ神父になって数年、二〇歳代の頃の話です。海で遭難したことがありました。夜釣りの最中、エンジンが故障して海峡の潮鞘に入ってしまったのです。季節風にあおられた波と激流で舟はままなりません。身も心も大自然と神に逆らっていたのです。「成るように成れ」後は神様まかせ。私は甲板に大の字になって寝てしまいました。

Chōwa suru
shizen wa kami ya
nowakinami

Making harmony
The work of nature God-like
Early autumn storm

It happened while I was in my 20s, only a few years after becoming a priest. I fell into trouble at sea. While fishing at night, my engine broke down, and I began drifting with the current flowing through the strait. The boat was at the mercy of the waves stirred by the seasonal windstorm and the strong current, and I couldn't fix the engine. Both physically and mentally, I felt I was fighting against nature and God. Resigning myself to the circumstances, I left everything to God, stretched out on the deck, and went to sleep.

ありがたや秋の潮さま夫婦舟

夜が明けると船は奈留島近くを漂流していました。一旦は満ち潮で沖に流されたものの、早朝には引き潮で奈留島附近に引き戻されたのです。「早朝ミサに神父様が来ない」と、信者さんの夫婦舟が全隻、私の捜索に出て来ました。

Arigata ya
aki no shio sama
meotobune

So grateful for them!
The autumn tide's ebb and flow
And mom-and-pop boats

With dawn, I discovered that I was drifting in the vicinity of Narushima Island. In the high tide, the boat had been pushed out into the open sea for a while, but the ebb tide in the early morning had pulled it back near Narushima. The people had become worried when I did not show up for mass, and all of the mom-and-pop boats were out looking for me.

Note: Narushima Island is located in the Goto Archipelago.

芋煮えて椿油の香ばしさ

お鍋で芋がグツグツと音をたてています。おいしそうな匂いです。椿油の香り、次の料理の準備でしょうか。五島では魚介類も野菜も米、味噌そして椿油もすべて自給自足です。

Imo niete
tsubakiabura no
kōbashisa

**Taros being stewed
In oil of camellia
What an aroma!**

The taros are gurgling in the kettle as they stew. The smell is appetizing. It is the aroma of camellia oil. Perhaps the cook is making preparations for the next meal. In the Goto Islands, the seafood, vegetables, miso bean paste, and even camellia oil are all locally produced.

馬小屋に門松のある御堂かな

私は、日本風の馬小屋を造ってもらい門口に似合った門松を飾ることを好みます。日本風（門）の新しいキリストを、新しいキリスト者になることを待つ（松）意味で。

Umagoya ni
kadomatsu no aru
midō kana

The stable waiting
Festooned with New Year's
pine sprigs
Hirado churches

I like to have a Japanese-style stable and decorate it with pine sprigs (a traditional New Year's decoration), which look good on the gate. The meaning is that I am "waiting" for a Japanese-style (gate) new Christ and the birth of new Christians. (The Japanese words for "wait" and "pine" are homonyms.)

アゴだしのスープはいかがザビエル殿

ザビエルが宣教でおとずれた平戸では、宿主の木村家が真っ先に洗礼を受けています。もしかしたら平戸の名産品、アゴのだしが効いたスープを差し上げたかもしれませんね。

Agodashi no
sūpu wa ikaga
zabieru dono

How about some soup
Made with broth from flying fish,
Father Xavier?

- Commentary:At Hirado, which Xavier visited on his mission, the Kimura family, who ran the inn where he stayed, were the first to be baptized. It could possibly be that they served him some soup made with broth from flying fish, a Hirado specialty.

人ごみにナフタリンの香復活祭

　母の実家は江袋教会のほんの隣でした。子どものころよく泊まりに行きました。復活祭ともなると、みんなが一張羅を着てくるのです。きっと箪笥から出したてだったのでしょう。ナフタリンの香りを懐かしく想い出します。

Hitogomi ni
nafutarin no ka
fukkatsusai

The crowd of faithful
All scented with naphthalene
On Easter Sunday

My mother's family home was located almost right next to Ebukuro Church. As a child, I often went there and stayed overnight. When Easter arrived, we all put on our Sunday best. The clothes had surely just been taken out of the dresser; I fondly remember how they smelled of mothballs.

東京にも子どもの五月あったんだ

「智恵子抄」に「東京に青い空があった」という一節があります。五月のこどもの日の大都会東京。元気に遊ぶ子どもらの姿を見ていますと、何かホッとします。

Tōkyō ni mo
kodomo no gogatsu
atta n da

So in Tokyo too
They celebrate Children's Day
On the fifth of May

The "Portrait of Chieko" (a collection of poems by Kotaro Takamura) contains the verse "There was a blue sky in Tokyo." It was the fifth of May, Children's Day, in the huge metropolis of Tokyo. Watching the children gleefully playing made me feel reassured.

峠より海の底まで帰省かな

久し振りの帰省。「ふるさとは遠きにありて思ふもの」と思っていました。しかし、「ふるさとは久しぶり来て思うもの」と悟りました。峠から見るふるさとは海の底まで思い出が。

Tōge yori
umi no soko made
kisei kana

**From the mountain pass
To the bottom of the sea
The homeward journey**

My first trip back home in a long time. I used to think that a hometown was something to recall from afar. But I realized that it is something to ponder when visiting after a long absence. The hometown viewed from a pass conjures up memories. And I could even see the bottom of the sea!

日曜のミサよりサザエ獲りたしや

日曜日の朝、ミサを捧げながら心は海にあります。サザエの姿が浮かびます。子どもの頃の不信仰な業が蘇ってきました。まだ信仰が足りませんね。

Nichiyō no

misa yori sazae

tori tashi ya

More than Sunday mass
By going turbo hunting
The boy's mind captured

Even as I say Mass on Sunday morning, my mind wanders to the sea and pictures turban shells. I remember my impious behavior as a boy. I guess my devotion is still insufficient.

Note: The horned turban, Turbo cornutus, is a sea mollusk considered a delicacy in Japan.

輪番の夫婦舟から桜鯛

久賀島の浜脇教会にいた頃の話です。この教会では八隻の夫婦舟が輪番で教会の神父の食卓の魚をとっていました。教会の桜が満開になると教会下の波止場に色鮮やかな桜鯛が水揚げされます。美しくもありがたい風景です。

Rimban no
meotobune kara
sakuradai

Going out in turns
Mom-and-pop boats bring bounty
Tasty cherry bass

It was when I was at Hamawaki Church on Hisakajima Island. At that church, eight mom-and-pop boats take turns going out to catch fish for the pastor's dinner table. When the cherry trees are in full bloom, vividly colored cherry bass are taken off the boats at the dock below the church. They make a striking and welcome sight.

伊勢海老を「ガンジ」と名付く神父かな

ある夏の日、禁漁期なのに大きな伊勢海老が網に掛かりました。海に戻したところで死んでしまいます。私は「大きなガンジ（カニ）がかかったから貰って帰るよ」と、持ち帰って食べました。これって密漁ではありませんよね。（五島の久賀島では、「カニ」のことを「ガンジ」と言っていました。）

Ise ebi o
ganji to nazuku
shimpu kana

A giant lobster
That bore the name of Gandhi
Christened by a priest

One summer day, a large lobster was caught in a net before the season for catching them had come. It would die if returned to the sea. I said, "We netted a big Gandhi, so let's take it with us." So we took it back to shore, cooked it, and ate it. I hope this doesn't fall in the category of poaching. (On the island of Hisakajima, one of the Goto Islands, people used to call crabs "ganji.")

烏賊墨の一筋垂れて冬の弥撒

早朝のミサの寄せ鐘で、あわてて烏賊漁から教会に戻ってミサを挙げました。ミサが終わる信者さんたちがクスクス笑い私の額を指差します。烏賊のスミがあったのです。

Ikasumi no
hitosuji tarete
fuyu no misa

I rush back to port
Wearing a streak of squid ink
Winter morning mass

Hearing the ring of the bell calling people to the early morning mass, I swiftly came back from fishing for squid, went into the church, and said Mass. When the service was finished, some of the worshippers pointed at my forehead, snickering. It was stained with squid ink.

青天のへきれきのごと降臨祭

二〇一八年五月二〇日、午後八時過ぎ、突然、「枢機卿親任おめでとうございます」との電話。何の前触れもなく、大騒ぎになってしまいました。戸惑いを通り過ぎて、こんなことが起こりうるのかと不審に思いました。聖霊降臨祭の日ではある、「青天のへきれき」とはこういうことなのでしょうか。

Seiten no

hekireki no goto

kōrinsai

Sudden the message
Like a bolt out of the blue
Feast of Pentecost

At a little after 8:00 p.m. on May 20, 2018, I suddenly received a telephone call congratulating me on my appointment as a new cardinal. I had had no inkling of this, and the call caused considerable commotion. I was beyond bewilderment, and couldn't believe that such a thing could happen. It was the Feast of the Pentecost. A real bolt out of the blue.

仕合わせの網を降ろすや海の日に

枢機卿親任発表から二週間後、二人の補佐司教が発表された。補佐司教叙階式と親任発表ミサを七月一六日の海の日に行いました。二人の補佐司教と「お互いに生かし合い、大切にし合い、仕え合って」、仕合わせになろうとの句です。

Shiaswase no
ami o orosuya
umi no hi ni

Lowering the net
For a haul of happiness
Mass on Marine Day

Two weeks after the announcement of my appointment as a cardinal came a notice of two auxiliary bishops to assist me. The ordination ceremony for these bishops and mass for my new appointment were held on July 16th, which was Marine Day, one of the Japanese holidays. I and the two bishops promised to support, cherish, and serve each other. This haiku expresses our shared desire to be happy in the relationship.

パパ様の離日寂しく時雨けり

二〇一九年一一月二三日から二六日まで、教皇フランシスコが来日されました。「すべてのいのちを守るため」、「あなたに話がある！」との感動的な訪日でした。羽田空港からの離日の時は、冷たい冬時雨が、寂しさを募りました。「いつまで立っているのか、今度はあなた方が、『すべてのいのちを守るため』行きなさい」とご示唆をのこされたのでしょうか。

Papa sama no
rinichi sabishiku
shigurekeri

The Pope's departure
Making the sadness deeper
Late autumnal rain

Pope Francis visited Japan from the 23rd to the 26th of November 2019. It was a very moving visit. He called for "protecting all life" and proclaimed that he had a message for us. When it was time for his plane to depart from Haneda Airport, a cold rain of the kind that falls in late autumn in Japan made me feel even sadder about his leaving. I thought: "How long are you going to stand there? Now it is your turn to take action 'to protect all life."

補遺の一句（黒田杏子選）

夕立の打ちたる海の青さかな

長崎の西海橋を車で走っている時でした。突然の激しい雨に前が見えなくなりました。数分後、海は洗い流されたように真っ青に見えたのです。

Supplementary haiku selected by Momoko Kuroda

yūdachi no
uchi taru umi no
aosa kana

Sudden evening squall
The sea pelted with raindrops
Now a bluer blue

It was when I was driving over the Saikai Bridge in Nagasaki. It abruptly began to rain so hard that I could not see through the windshield. A few minutes later, and the sea had turned deep blue, as if its cloudiness had been washed away by the rain.

前田万葉句集

解説にかえて

黒田杏子

Haiku of Manyo Maeda

Commentary

Momoko Kuroda

手許にとどいた句稿は五十句。
どの句も炊きたてのごはんのように、また窯で焼き上げたばかりのパンのように、香りたち新鮮。たっぷりと存在感があり、読み手のこころにすっと響いてくる親しみやすい作品でした。
頭の中で構築された言葉の組合せはどの句にも全く無く、すべて作者のこころと身体がじかに感じとった純真無垢とも言うべき表現の作品が揃っています。
何度か読み返してみましたが、この感想は変りません。
長い年月、句作に励み、届けられる数多くの句集に目を通してきた私ですが、これほど読後の印象が爽やかで、ゆたかな、ここちよい気分に満たされたことは無かったのです。
句稿を拝見する前に、私は旧知の「かまくら春秋社」代表の伊藤玄二郎さんから、この作者の著書『烏賊墨の一筋垂れて冬の弥撒』をお贈り頂いてをり、加えて若いときから長崎県の各地、とくに五島列島の島々を句作の吟行地としてかなり歩いていたこと、さらにキリシタン史についてもそれなりの情報を手にしておりました。それでこの本をとても興味深く完読させていただいておりました。
そして去る三月二日、ゆくりなくも私は前田万葉枢機卿にじかにお目にかかる機会を頂いたのです。

伊藤さんプロデュースの「俳句を語る」座談会。句友の俊英俳人夏井いつきさん。親友の経済人でエッセイストの古川洽次さんとご一緒に枢機卿と座を共にさせて頂きました。

これまで私は何人かの外国人の神父様にはお目にかかったことがありましたが、日本人の大司教・枢機卿というお立場の方にお目にかかったことはありませんでした。

前田万葉というご本名と俳名を持たれるこのお方の第一印象は「海の男」。現役の漁師顔負けの体躯。見るからにたくましいお方でしたが、その話しぶりと表情は私に「慈愛」という日本語を久々に憶い出させて下さったお方でもありました。

私はこの五十句の中から、次の八句をとりわけこころに残る句として抄出させて頂きます。一句一句の解説や鑑賞は、作者ご自身がすべての作品に自句自解を添えておられますので、あえて記しません。私はこの八句について私の共感のこころを短く書きとどめ、この句集に遭遇できた歓びを皆さまにお伝えしたいと思います。

母の日や母から母へまた母へ

たっぷりと母上様の愛情につつまれて育ったお方でなければ、一行の中に「母」の文字を四回も散りばめることは出来ません。

うしろ手に母のまねして麦を踏む

自画像でしょう。万葉少年のこの姿の愛らしさ。麦の芽を踏む母と子の絆がいきいきと詠み上げられていて、涙ぐましくもなります。

ごきげんよう夫婦燕の宙返り

燕の夫婦にこれほどまでに慕われる司教様。「ごきげんよう」の六音字のあっせんが圧巻ですね。この作者の身に備わった「いきもの感覚」は抜群。人間と燕。そのいのちの交歓が涙ぐましいまでの一行です。

馬小屋に門松のある御堂かな

私の生家は代々神道でした。この句に接して、子供時代に親しんだクリスマスの物語の絵本やカードの画像などをとても懐かしく思い出しました。この御堂の前に立ってみたいとも思ったことでした。

輪番の夫婦舟から桜鯛

たったいま海から上ったばかりの桜鯛がとどけられる。何と豊かな幸せな人生。夫婦舟からというところもめでたいですね。捧げる人も受けとる方も、笑顔いっぱい……。信者と神父。このような人間関係の存在を初めて知りました。虹色に輝く魚体。心躍る、無限に心の拡がってゆく華麗な句です。

烏賊墨の一筋垂れて冬の弥撒

「漁師神父」と自称・自任される作者の面目躍如たる句。ユーモア、滑稽は俳句の大切な要素です。それはまた知力体力に恵まれ、弁舌さわやかなお方のたのもしい武器ともなりましょう。

仕合わせの網を降ろすや海の日に

聖書に記された言葉をそのままいかされて成った一行十七音字の作品。「海の日」という季語のあっせんもこの句に太陽の恵みを感じさせ、明るく重厚な奥行きを加えているように思われます。

夕立の打ちたる海の青さかな

季語の現場に立って詠み上げられた句には鮮度と臨場感があって魅了されます。写実句の強みがよく出ている作品です。大夕立のあとの海原の青さ。読者の身も心も洗い浄められてゆきます。

俳句は世界最短の詩。ミニマム故にマキシマムな世界を創造できるのだと年ごとに私は実感するようになってきています。

まことに俳句の五七五は世界に誇ってよい形式であると考えます。

この日本の国民文芸「俳句」にいま、地球上のあらゆる人々の関心が寄せられています。すでに「俳句」は「ＨＡＩＫＵ」として、世界の共通語となりました。インターネットやメールでこの瞬間も作品が自在にやりとりされています。

その昔、「老年の文芸」ともいわれていた俳句。現在は幼児から百歳を超す長寿者の方々まで、年齢にかかわりなく、いきいきと日々作品を生み出しているのです。

ところで小説家で仏教者の九八歳の現役作家瀬戸内寂聴さんは私の主宰する俳句結社「藍生」の創刊以来のメンバーです。先年、はじめての句集『ひとり』を刊行され、国民的話題を集めています。彼女は一貫して反戦の意思を表明。その意志を句にも詠み、さまざまな平和を守る活動をすすめてきておられます。

前田万葉枢機卿も一貫して強く世界の平和を希い、祈っておられることを知りました。

一九四五年、昭和二十年に、疎開先の栃木県南那須の村で小学生となり、八月に終戦日を迎えた私も、一人の市民として俳人として反戦の立場に立ち、この国と世界の平和を強く希求しております。

このたび、ゆくりなくも前田万葉枢機卿と句縁を賜り、親しくお目にかかる機会を与えて頂きました。そして初めての御句集に言葉を添える機会を与えられました。誠に光栄に存じます。

俳人は全員平等です。「俳諧自由」の精神がこのたびの『前田万葉句集』の刊行を機に、この地球上に一層拡がり、浸透してゆくことを信じ、そのことを心より希い、祈っております。

二〇二〇年四月十五日

And on March 2, I was unexpectedly given the opportunity to meet Cardinal Manyo Maeda myself.

The occasion was a symposium titled "Talking About Haiku" produced by Ito. I met Cardinal Maeda along with the distinguished fellow haiku poet Itsuki Natsui and Koji Furukawa, a close friend who is both a businessman and essayist.

Previously, I had made the acquaintance of several non-Japanese priests, but had never met a Japanese cleric with the position of archbishop or cardinal.

My first impression of the cardinal, who uses his real name Manyo Maeda for his pen name as well, was that he was "a man of the sea." He had a better build than a professional fisherman. He looked burly as could be, but the way he talked and the look on his face called to mind the Japanese word "jiai" ("benevolence") for the first time in what had been a long while for me.

From this collection of fifty haiku, I have taken the liberty of selecting the following eight as those that especially abide in my heart. The poet has himself added his own comments on all of his haiku in this collection, and I will therefore not provide commentary and insights to assist appreciation of these eight. Instead, I will briefly remark on the feeling of empathy I conceived for each, in my desire to convey the joy I derived from encountering this anthology to all of its readers.

Commentary
- Momoko Kuroda

An anthology of 50 haiku delivered to my hands. Each emitting a refreshing fragrance, like freshly boiled rice or bread right out of the oven. Each has plenty of presence and an approachability that makes it gently strike a chord in the hearts of readers.

None of the haiku have any assemblages of words that were constructed in the mind; they all could be termed expressions of pure and genuine sentiments straight from the heart and body of the poet. This impression of mine has not changed even after reading them over several times.

For many years, I have written haiku and read many haiku collections that had been sent to me, but none has left me with such an invigorating impression and filled me with such a rich and pleasant feeling after reading as this one.

Before perusing the haiku, I received a complimentary copy of "Ikasumi no Hitosuji Tarete Fuyu no Misa," a book by the same poet, from Genjiro Ito, President of Kamakura Shunju Co. and an old friend of mine. In addition, from my youth, I have made some journeys to various spots in Nagasaki Prefecture, and particularly the Goto Islands, in search of inspiration. Furthermore, I have also obtained a considerable amount of information on the history of the Christians there. I consequently read this book from cover to cover with a great deal of interest.

* Going out in turns / Mom-and-pop boats bring bounty / Tasty cherry bass
- A catch of cherry bass just hauled from the sea. What a rich and happy life! The so-called "mom-and-pop" boats bringing it also carry the connotation of happiness. Both the giver and the receiver wearing big smiles... The faithful and their pastor. This was the first time I learned of the existence of this kind of interpersonal relationship. The fish with their gleaming reddish bodies. It is a dazzling haiku that makes the heart leap while widening it to limitless bounds.

* I rush back to port / Wearing a streak of squid ink / Winter morning mass
- This haiku paints a vivid picture of the poet, who calls himself a "fisherman-priest." Humor and wit are vital elements of haiku. They are also entertaining tools in the hands of those blessed with both intellectual power, physical strength, and an eloquent tongue.

* Lowering the net / For a haul of happiness / Mass on Marine Day
- A 17-kana poem that draws on words from the Bible. I believe that the season word "Marine Day," which fits the rest of the haiku nicely, makes the reader feel the bounty of the sun, and adds a bright and substantial depth to the haiku.

* Sudden evening squall / The sea pelted with raindrops / Now a bluer blue
- Born on the site of its season word, this haiku captivates the reader with its freshness and sense of being on the spot. It is a good demonstration of the power of realistic haiku. The deep blue of the

* Mother's Day arrives / Mother succeeding mother / Then comes another
- One who was not brought up generously wrapped in the love of his mother could use the word "mother" four times in the same haiku (in the Japanese original).

* Hands behind my back / Imitating my mother / Treading plants of wheat
- A picture which the poet painted of himself. A charming portrait of the boy Manyo. The bonds between mother and child are graphically described. It's enough to bring tears to my eyes.

* I bid a farewell / The swallow pair, taking wing / Somersault in air
- To think that a bishop felt this much affection for the swallow couple! The choice of the six-kana "gokigenyo" (literally "fare ye well," the first verse in the original) is a masterstroke. The person of the poet is equipped with an outstanding "creature feeling." A man and swallows. This friendly exchange between two different forms of life also makes me misty-eyed.

* The stable waiting / Festooned with New Year's pine sprigs / Hirado churches
- The family into which I was born has followed Shinto for generations. This haiku brought back fond childhood memories of things such as picture books about the story of Christmas and the pictures on Christmas cards.

her haiku, and is engaged in a variety of activities aimed at protecting peace.

I learned that Cardinal Maeda has likewise always had strong hopes for world peace and been praying for it.

In 1945, I entered elementary school in the village of Minami-Nasu in Tochigi Prefecture, where I had been evacuated during the war, and faced the end of the war there that August. As both a citizen and a haiku poet, I too have taken an anti-war stance and fervently seek peace for Japan and the world as a whole.

This time, I had the good fortune to become acquainted with Cardinal Maeda through haiku, be given the opportunity to meet him, and even be invited to make some comments on his first anthology of haiku. I feel truly honored by this involvement.

All haiku poets are equal. I believe that the publication of this "Manyo Maeda Haiku Collection" could spur the further spread and permeation of the spirit of haiku freedom throughout our planet, and earnestly hope and pray that it will indeed do so.

April 15, 2020

* Tentative translation.

sea after the heavy rains seems to cleanse and purify the reader, body and soul.

The haiku is the world's shortest poem. Year after year, it is brought home to me all over again that, precisely because of its minimal format, it can create a maximal world.

The 5-7-5 haiku is truly a poetry style of which Japan can boast to the rest of the world.

While it arose as one of Japan's popular literary genres, the haiku is now attracting the interest of all sorts of people across the globe. The very term "haiku" is now part of the vocabulary in languages around the world. At this very moment, haiku compositions are being freely exchanged through SNS and by email.

The haiku was once even regarded as a style of literary composition basically for the aged. But now, people of all ages, from the very young to the very old, are energetically producing works, day after day.

Jakucho Setouchi, the novelist and Buddhist nun who is still authoring new works at age 98, is one of the original members of the AOI haiku organization, which I lead, and has stayed with it since the very first issue of its journal. A few years ago, she came out with "Hitori" ("Lone"*), her first-ever haiku collection, which attracted nationwide attention. Throughout her life, she has always proclaimed her anti-war convictions. She likewise weaves these convictions into

前田　万葉（まえだ・まんよう）
1949年、長崎県新上五島町生まれ。カトリック大阪大司教区・大司教・枢機卿。1975年サン・スルピス大神学院卒業、司祭叙階。2011年司教叙階。2014年大司教着座。2018年枢機卿親任。祖母方の曾祖父一家はキリスト教弾圧時代に五島列島の久賀島で迫害され、3人が殉教。祖父はまだ偏見が強く残っていた時代にキリスト教に改宗。著書に『烏賊墨の一筋垂れて冬の弥撒』（かまくら春秋社）。

Manyo Maeda
Born in the town of Shin-Kamigoto, Nagasaki Prefecture in 1949, Manyo Maeda is Archbishop and Cardinal in the Catholic Archdiocese of Osaka. He was ordained a priest in 1975, upon his graduation from the Major Seminary of Saint Sulpice of Fukuoka. He was consecrated as bishop in 2011, and appointed to the position of archbishop in 2014 and cardinal in 2018. During the age of suppression of Christianity by the Tokugawa shogunate, the members of his great-grandfather's family on his grandmother's side were subjected to persecution, and three of them were martyred in Hisakajima, one of the Goto Islands. His grandfather converted to Christianity at a time when there was still deep prejudice against Christians. He is the author of "Ikasumi no Hitosuji Tarete Fuyu no Misa," (published by Kamakura Shunju-sha Co., Ltd).

前田万葉句集
2020年7月16日発行

著者 — 前田万葉
訳者 — ジェームス・ケティング
発行所 — かまくら春秋社
鎌倉市小町 2-14-7
0467-25-2864
発行人 — 伊藤玄二郎
印刷所 — ケイアール

Haiku of Manyo Maeda
Published July 16, 2020

Text by Manyo Maeda
Translated by James Koetting
Published by Kamakura Shunju-sha Co., Ltd
Address : 2-14-7 Komachi, Kamakura JAPAN
Tel : 0467-25-2864
Publisher : Genjiro Ito
Printed by KR, Ltd.,

ISBN978-4-7740-0812-7　C0092

前田万葉の本

烏賊墨（いかすみ）の一筋垂れて冬の弥撒（ミサ）

～万葉神父の日々是好日～

カトリック大阪大司教区・枢機卿
前田万葉 著

少年期は、「なぜ信者にしたのか」とか、神学生のころは、「なぜ神学校にやったのか」など、親への恨みを口にしたことがありました。しかし、今は、信者であってよかった、神父になってよかった、すべては親からの最高の贈り物、という感謝の思いで一杯です。　（「前田家の信仰遺産」より）

定価：本体1800円＋税
四六判　256ページ

アグネス・チャンさん 推薦！

前田万葉枢機卿様の言葉は「福音」です。その俳句と短歌には、神様の愛が宿っていて、読むものに大きな喜びを与えてくれます。
代々伝わる神様の愛を、ぜひこの一冊で感じて下さい。読んだ後、きっとより力強く、より安心して、喜びを抱きながら、日々を過ごす事が出来るはずです。

自作の俳句を織り交ぜながら、誰にでも分かるやさしい言葉で、温かく、ときに厳しく、福音を伝える前田万葉枢機卿。本書は、散逸していた 1988 年～ 2009 年の教会報を中心にまとめた「五七五便り」のほか、講演や対談を収録。厳しい迫害、偏見に遭う中、堅く信仰を守り続けた長崎・五島列島のキリシタンの末裔である枢機卿が語る、貴重な一冊。

かまくら春秋社　TEL 0467-25-2864 FAX 0467-60-1205　http://kamashun.co.jp